The Case of the
Class Clown

Read all the Jigsaw Jones Mysteries

Coming Soon

The Case of the Class Clown

by James Preller
illustrated by Jamie Smith
cover illustration by R. W. Alley

A
LITTLE APPLE
PAPERBACK

SCHOLASTIC INC.
New York Toronto London Auckland Sydney
Mexico City New Delhi Hong Kong

*For Mary Szczech (whose name I can't type without
spraining a finger), with thanks for providing me with a
"free pass" to her incredible, creative, happy classroom.
And, of course, thanks to all the children in Ms. Szczech's
1999–2000 classroom:*

*Katherine, Leanna, Jesse, Nicholas, Darien, Lily, Christopher,
Eliza, Grant, Evan, Jessica, Kathleen, Sasha, Jacob, Connor,
Kayla, Jillian, Daniel, Danielle, Brian, Kristen, and Karen.*

You guys are awesome!
—J. P.

Book design by Dawn Adelman

ISBN 0-439-18474-6

24 23 22 21 20 19 18 17   5/0

Printed in the U.S.A.   40
First Scholastic printing, November 2000

CONTENTS

Chapter One
Slimed

You might say that Athena Lorenzo and I had a friendship right out of a picture book. Only I was a little pig and she was the big bad wolf.

Yeesh.

We sat together in my tree house after school. Actually, I sat. Athena was too mad to sit. Instead she huffed and puffed until steam poured out of her ears. She gritted her teeth. She waved her fists. She stomped her feet until the tree house shook.

"Hey, watch it," I complained. "This tree

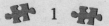 1

house isn't made of bricks, you know. That's the little piggy down the road."

Athena suddenly stopped. She gazed at me through large, round eyes. "Say what? The piggy next door?"

"The Three Little Pigs," I explained. "You know, one little piggy built his house with bricks. One used sticks. And the laziest little piggy used straw." I rapped my knuckles on the tree house. "These walls aren't made of bricks. Get it? I don't care

how much you huff and puff, Athena. Just don't blow my tree house down."

Athena's eyes narrowed. "You're strange," she observed.

"*I'm* strange?" I protested. "That's a laugh. You're the one who's acting crazy." I handed Athena a cup of grape juice. "Drink this. It might calm you down."

I leaned back on my hands and watched Athena slurp the juice. She had dark, round eyes and thick eyebrows. Her hair was a tangle of knots and whirls. I thought about why she was here. And I had to smile. It was going to be one of my *stickiest* cases ever.

After all, it began with green slime.

Squishy, squashy, ooey, gooey slime.

It was my job to find out who left it in Athena's gym sneaker. I'm a detective. For a dollar a day, I make problems go away. And Athena Lorenzo had a problem, all right.

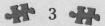 3

Squish, squash. Slimy socks!

"Stop smiling," Athena barked. "It's not funny."

I bit my lip and tried not to smile. "It is sort of funny," I argued. "I mean, when you put your foot in that sneaker . . . and the slime oozed out . . . and you yelled, 'I'VE BEEN SLIMED!' I've never heard so much laughter in my life!"

Just then my partner, Mila, climbed up the tree house. As usual, she was singing. I recognized the tune. It was one of those golden oldies songs that my father's always playing. But Mila changed the words around:

"Who's that girl just a-climbing up the tree?
Singing do-wah-ditty, ditty-dum, ditty-do!
She's got a new case and she needs a clue.
Singing do-wah-ditty, ditty-dum, ditty-do!"

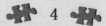

Mila plopped down beside me, cross-legged. "Did I miss much?"

I jerked my thumb toward Athena. "She was having a cow, that's about it."

"What do you mean, having a cow?" Athena asked.

"A temper tantrum," I explained. "That's your problem, Athena. You've got to lighten up. What's the big deal, anyway? Somebody pulled a prank. Just think of it as an April Fools' joke."

"This is November," Athena moaned.

"So? It came early. Big whoop," I sympathized.

"Yeah," Mila chimed in. "It was just harmless fun, Athena. And you've got to admit it. Everybody thought it was *soooo* funny."

"Not me," Athena shot back. "I think someone has a pretty rotten sense of humor. One minute I'm getting dressed for gym class. The next minute I've got a foot full of slime!"

I smiled at the memory.

"Don't smile," Athena demanded. "It *wasn't* funny. When everybody laughed, I felt embarrassed."

Mila pulled on her long black hair. She nodded. "I see what you mean, Athena. Nobody likes to be laughed at." Mila turned to me. "Let's catch this clown, Jigsaw."

I caught Athena's eye and nodded

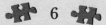

toward a glass jar. *Ka-ching, kachink.* She dropped in a handful of change.

I opened my detective journal to a clean page. I grinned. "OK, this shouldn't be so tough. After all, how hard can it be to find a clown? All we've got to do is look for somebody with a red nose and big floppy shoes."

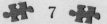

Chapter Two
Eating Socks

"No more jokes," Athena threatened. "Or I'll pour grape juice over your head."

I glared at Athena. This case was five minutes old, and she was already bugging me. "Look, Athena. If you want my help, you have to play by the rules. Rule number one: *No messing with the grape juice.*"

I winked at her. Slowly, the corners of Athena's mouth turned up. "I'm sorry," she apologized. "But it makes me crazy. I can't believe someone put slime in my sneaker."

"I understand," Mila said gently. "Do you

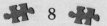 8

have any idea who might have done this?"

Athena shook her head.

"Is anyone mad at you?"

A shrug. "Nope."

"No idea at all?"

Athena brushed some hair from her face. "No idea," she said.

"Think, Athena," I urged. "Did you notice any clues at all?"

Athena reached into her back pocket. She took out a small piece of brown paper. She laid it on the floor, smoothing it with long, thin fingers. "I found this in my cubby."

The note had one word, in fat letters:

I placed the paper inside a plastic bag. "Our first clue," I noted. "Was there anything with it?"

"No, nothing else."

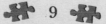

"How about the socks?" I asked. "Do you still have 'em?"

"They're in my backpack," Athena said. "I'm taking them home to be washed. Why?"

"Evidence," Mila said.

"That's right," I agreed. "We'll need to keep the socks. They might be clues."

Athena raised an eyebrow. "You want my smelly old gym socks? They're covered with green slime."

I held open a plastic bag. I explained, "Mysteries are like jigsaw puzzles. Every piece is important."

Holding the socks by her fingertips, Athena dropped them in the bag. I began to zip it closed. "Wait," Mila cried. "Taste the socks first."

I scoffed. "I am *not* tasting Athena's socks. You taste 'em."

To my surprise, Mila leaned forward to sniff the bag. Finally, she dabbed her finger

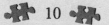

into a glob of slime. Then she brought it to the tip of her tongue.

And licked.

"Disgusting," Athena complained.

Mila dabbed again. She held her green-tipped finger to my face. "You try it," she offered.

"No, thanks," I replied. "I've already eaten."

Mila sucked on her finger and smiled. "Jell-O," she announced. "Lime Jell-O."

"Really?" I dabbed at the sock and tasted it myself. "Hey, that's pretty good."

 11

Chapter Three

The Raisin Circus

Athena left a few minutes later.

"Let's talk inside," I told Mila. We walked to the house. I held open the back door leading into the kitchen. "I'm worried about something."

"Worried?" Mila asked as she stepped inside. "What are you . . . ?"

Mila stopped cold in her tracks. I almost bumped into her from behind. We stood and gaped at my father. He was sitting at the kitchen table, talking to a pile of

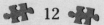

raisins. That's right — *talking*. We heard him say, "Listen here, you dried-up grapes. I need you to concentrate."

"Hi, Mr. Jones!" Mila cried. "What are you doing?"

My dad glanced up, with a surprised look on his face. He threw a napkin over the raisins and picked up the newspaper. "Oh, er, hi. I didn't hear you kids come in."

"Were you talking . . . *to the raisins*?" Mila asked.

My dad's cheeks turned pink. "Talking to raisins? Whatever gave you that idea?"

I lifted up the napkin, revealing a handful of raisins. "We heard you," I said.

"Oh — *THOSE RAISINS*," he exclaimed, snapping his fingers. "We weren't talking, exactly." He shifted in his chair. "Don't you kids have anything to do?"

I shook my head.

"No homework? Dog walked?" he asked.

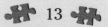

"Dad," I said. "*Why* were you talking to raisins?!"

My dad looked around the room. He cupped his hand around his mouth and whispered, "I'm *training* them."

"You're what?"

"Training them," he repeated. "You've heard of the flea circus? Well, I'm starting a raisin circus."

I groaned. My dad loved practical jokes. I knew he was up to something. Only I didn't know what.

"A raisin circus?" Mila repeated, as if she hadn't heard correctly.

"That's right," he replied. "Just a few easy tricks. Nothing special."

I pulled Mila by the elbow. "Let's get out of here, Mila. We've got work to do."

Mila yanked her arm away. "Wait, Jigsaw." She eyed my father carefully. "What kind of tricks?"

He sighed. "I'm not sure yet. I'd like to

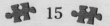

teach them how to jump," he said. "I figure if Mexican jumping beans can do it, why not raisins?"

"Don't listen to him, Mila," I urged. "It's just another one of his jokes. Let's go downstairs."

My dad winked. "Don't worry, Mila. I'll invite you to the show after I get these bad boys trained."

Mila and I left my father alone at the kitchen table. "Your dad's funny," Mila observed.

"Funny how?" I asked. "Funny ha-ha? Or funny strange?"

Mila shrugged. "Both, I guess."

Oh, brother.

We grabbed a few cookies and went down to my basement. "Okay," Mila said. "What's got you so worried?"

Chapter Four
Phony Bologna

I opened my journal. I wrote:

The Case of the Class Clown.

Mila looked over my shoulder. "That's not a good name. We should call it The Case of the Smelly Socks."

I disagreed. "Think about it, Mila. Putting Jell-O in Athena's sneaker was a joke. Right? So who makes jokes?"

"Jim Carrey," Mila answered.

"Alrighty then!" I replied, doing my best Ace Ventura impression. "But what *type* of person makes jokes?"

Mila paused. "A comedian."

"Right," I said. "Or a clown."

"So."

"So," I said. "Who's the class clown in room 201?"

"That's easy," Mila answered. "Ralphie Jordan. He's always messing around."

"Exactly," I said. "It's got to be him. But I can't rat on Ralphie. He's one of my best friends."

Mila thought it over. "We're detectives, Jigsaw. Athena hired us to solve the mystery. We've got to catch the prankster — no matter *who* it is."

Mila was right. She knew it. I knew it. But I didn't have to like it. Not one bit. After all, who wants to be a tattletale? Not Jigsaw Jones, that's for sure.

"Don't worry, Jigsaw. We're not even sure it's Ralphie. It could be anybody."

"Could be," I said, doubtfully.

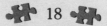

Mila looked at me firmly. "You'll do the right thing."

"That's what worries me," I muttered.

Suddenly my father's voice boomed down the stairs. "Mila! Your stepmother, Alice, just called. She wants you home right now. You're late for a piano lesson."

"Oh, my gosh!" Mila exclaimed, jumping to her feet. "I've gotta go, Jigsaw. See you in school tomorrow!"

Later that night, I got a phone call from Joey Pignattano. He was all worked up. "I need a detective, Jigsaw. It's an emergency! Somebody's out to get me!"

"Slow down," I said. "Take a deep breath and tell me all about it."

"I was almost poisoned!" Joey said.

"Poisoned?!"

"Yeah — *to death*! It happened at school today. In the cafeteria. I took a bite out of my bologna sandwich and tasted something *strange*."

"That's what you get for eating bologna," I said. "They don't call it mystery meat for nothing."

"Stop joking," Joey objected. "This is serious. When I opened my sandwich, I found out that somebody had put in rubber bologna!"

"Rubber bologna?"

"Yeah," Joey said. "Phony bologna."

I'd seen the stuff before. You could buy

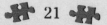

it at The Party Store in the Jokes and Gags section. It was right next to the fake throw-up.

"Any other clues?" I asked.

"Yeah," Joey said. "I found a brown piece of paper inside my lunch box. There was writing on it —"

I interrupted him. "Let me guess. It said, 'Gotcha!'"

Joey was impressed. "Wow, how'd *you* know?"

I yawned. "I'm a detective, Joey. Trouble is my business."

That night, I took a long, hot bath. I lay perfectly still, thinking about my good pal Ralphie Jordan. It sounded like the kind of pranks he'd pull. I put my head under the water and counted as high as I could. When I came up for air, I knew two things: Catching Ralphie wouldn't be easy. And it wouldn't be fun.

Some days, being a detective was the toughest job in town. I ducked my head under the water again. For some reason, I liked things better down there.

Chapter Five

Two Lies

The next morning, Mila and I slid into our bus seats. I told her about Joey's call.

"Do you really think it's Ralphie?" Mila asked.

"Probably," I replied. "But whoever did this had to get into Athena's gym bag and Joey's lunch box — without anyone seeing."

Mila rocked back and forth, thinking. "The cubbies!" she exclaimed. "That's where our gym clothes and lunch boxes are stored."

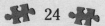 24

In Ms. Gleason's class, everybody had different jobs. One of the jobs was keeping the cubbies neat. I told Mila, "Find out who was on cubby patrol this week. Maybe they saw something."

Mila nodded. "You got it, Jigsaw."

Ralphie Jordan suddenly popped his head up from the seat in front of us. "Hey, guys! What are you talking about?"

My heart skipped a beat.

Mila stammered, "Er, uh . . . well . . ."

"Homework!" I lied, a little too loudly. "We were talking about homework."

I felt guilty about lying to Ralphie — as if I'd just drowned his pet goldfish.

"Bah, homework!" Ralphie said, making a face. "Forget that! Let's talk about Athena. Wasn't it awesome when she put her foot in that slime? I nearly died laughing."

I didn't feel right hanging around with Ralphie. I was a detective — and he was my number one suspect. It wasn't time to pal around. Just then, the bus pulled up in front of school. I grabbed my pack and hustled off. I was feeling worse than ever. Ralphie was one of my best friends. But now I couldn't look him in the eye.

I was almost glad when Helen Zuckerman cornered me on the way to class. Lately, Helen had been acting a little weird. I mean, even *weirder* than usual. She had been reading a lot of joke books. Then she told corny jokes all day.

Here's the thing. For some reason, Helen Zuckerman had decided to *become* funny. Which is sort of like deciding to become a tall redhead. Some things you just *can't change*. And Helen Zuckerman, no matter how hard she tried, was about as funny as a spelling test.

"Hey, Jigsaw. Why do ghosts hear so well?"

 27

I shrugged.

"Because they're eerie!" Helen snorted and burst out laughing.

I groaned.

"Get it?" she said. "*Eerie?* Like, you know, ears!"

I told her I got it.

"Here's another one," she said.

I started to walk away.

Helen grabbed me by the shoulder. "What kind of books do skunks read?"

"Dunno," I said.

"Best-*smellers*!" Helen howled.

What a stinker. I forced myself to smile.

Helen frowned. "You don't think I'm funny, do you?" Her lower lip trembled. Her face twitched. I could see she was upset.

"Well," I began, "it's just that . . ."

Helen looked at me hopefully.

I couldn't tell her the truth. It would hurt her feelings too much. I finally said, "The

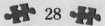

thing is . . . I heard that joke before. Maybe I'd laugh if you told me another one."

"Really?" Helen asked. "OK. Why did the principal . . . whoops, I messed that up. Sorry! Why did the *vampire* get sent to the principal's office?"

"I give up."

"He had a bat attitude! Get it — *bat* attitude! Like, *bad* attitude. But it's *bat* attitude!"

I could have won an award for best actor. I giggled. I snickered. I snorted. I laughed until my throat hurt. "Bwwwaaaa-haaaa-haaaa!" I screamed. "That's *sooooo* funny!"

Sure, it was a lie. But at least it made Helen smile. I guess lying is OK sometimes. I think. Maybe.

Cubbie Patrol:
Ralphie Jordan

Chapter Six
Drop Everything and Laugh

Ms. Gleason clapped her hands softly, *clap – clap*. That was our signal to be quiet. We all clapped back, *CLAP – CLAP – CLAP*.

Ms. Gleason smiled. "Good morning, boys and girls. I love it when you listen for my signals."

She wiped her hand across her forehead. "Wow, what a morning! My crazy basset hound, Brutus, got loose again. You should have seen me. I was in my bathrobe, chasing Brutus through my neighbor's garden!"

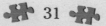

We all laughed. We loved it when Ms. Gleason told us her Brutus stories. Her dog sounded like a real nut. One time, Brutus even ate Ms. Gleason's new shoes!

We began each day by reading our daily letter aloud. Every morning, Ms. Gleason wrote a letter and put a copy on all our desks. At 10:30, we were going to meet with our fifth-grade buddies. In the afternoon, Eddie Becker's grandmother was coming in to read us a story.

Ms. Gleason said, "Meeting Eddie's grandmother will be a lot of fun. I know you will be a polite audience. Remember, pay attention, listen carefully, and be *observant.* You'll write about the story in your journals when she leaves."

For language arts, Ms. Gleason needed help fixing some sentences that were broken. She called me up to the easel. There were two sentences written on it:

that boy don't go to
pottsford school any more

ms willard will learn us how to
multiply this year said irving

It was my job to put in the right punctuation and correct the mistakes. No biggie. Ms. Gleason let me call on other students for help. I liked that. It made me feel like a teacher. I called on Danika

 33

Starling first. She knew the right answer to everything.

In no time at all, we made the sentences as good as new.

that boy doesn't go to

Pottsford School anymore.

"Ms. Willard will teach us how to

multiply this year," said Irving.

After that, we had DEAR time. That's when we had to Drop Everything And Read. We weren't supposed to *drop* anything, actually. But that didn't stop Ralphie Jordan. Every day at DEAR time,

he threw something on the ground and hollered, "Look out below!"

We usually laughed. Only this time he dropped a heavy book on Geetha Nair's toe. So it wasn't funny. Geetha was furious. She scolded Ralphie, "You should never mess around with somebody else's toes."

And I guess that made sense.

Sort of. In a weird way.

At lunch, Mila came up to me. "Bad news," she said. "I checked the bulletin

board. Ralphie is on Cubby Patrol this week."

"What about the handwriting?" I asked Mila. "Did you compare the notes to Ralphie's handwriting?"

Mila shrugged. "It's not the same, but that doesn't mean anything. The notes were written in a special way. Nobody writes in fat letters all the time. It would take forever."

I nodded glumly. "This case just keeps getting worse and worse. Look what's for dessert this week." I pointed to my lunch tray. On a small plate sat a shivering pile of lime Jell-O.

I didn't much feel like eating it.

Go figure.

Chapter Seven
The Fish Tank Prank

There were two more pranks on Thursday. I was standing right there when the first one happened. It was a whopper. Mila nearly jumped out of her socks.

When we start the day, we come into the classroom in dribs and drabs. Ms. Gleason's usually out in the hall, chatting with some kids or another teacher. We talk to one another, put our backpacks away, mess around. Until the bell rings, we're pretty much free to do what we want.

"Hey, what's this?" Mila said, surprised.

There was a small round tin on her desk. It had a bow on it. "A present? It's not my birthday."

Mila picked it up. She began to twist it open . . .

I suddenly got a bad feeling. "Wait!" I shouted.

Too late. Another twist and — *sploing!* — some springy snakes shot out of the can and sprang into the air. "ACK!" Mila screamed, nearly falling over a chair.

"Bwaaaa-haaaa-ha, haaa-haaa!" Everyone who saw it laughed. Mila bent down to pick up a piece of brown paper that popped out of the can. She read it, grumbled, and shoved it in her desk.

In the confusion, Athena came up to me. "Any suspects?" she asked.

I glanced around the classroom. My eyes landed on Ralphie, who was laughing hysterically with Eddie Becker.

"Nope," I said coldly.

"None?" Athena asked, eyes wide. "Not one suspect?!"

"Nope!" I snapped. "Not one."

"I thought you were some kind of great detective," Athena growled. "What's the matter? Is this case too hard for you?"

I wiggled two fingers in the air. "Rule number two: *No bugging the detective.*"

I walked away without looking back. This prankster was starting to get on my nerves.

Out on the playground, Mila tried to

cheer me up. "Don't worry, Jigsaw. It was just a joke. I'm not mad or anything. It's no big deal, really."

I forced a smile. "Sure. *No big deal.* That's probably what the turkeys said about the first Thanksgiving."

When we got back from afternoon recess, Bigs Maloney was the first person to notice it. From the doorway, he pointed at the fish tank. "LOOK! The water's PINK!"

And it sure was.

Pink as cotton candy.

Not that our goldfish — Elmer, Bugs, and Daffy — seemed to mind. They just happily swam around, *glub, glub, glub.* Goldfish are like that. They don't care whether they live in an Olympic-size swimming pool or a toilet bowl.

Everybody was excited and alarmed. Well, not everybody. I thought Nicole Rodriguez was going to cry. She was a real animal lover. "The poor little fish," she kept saying. "The poor little fish."

"Chill out," snapped Bobby Solofsky. "It's probably just food coloring. I put it on my Rice Krispies all the time."

Lucy Hiller found a note taped to the side of the tank. It was the same brown paper. The same balloonlike letters. The same message: **GOTCHA!**

"Boys, girls, sit down!" Ms. Gleason ordered. You could tell from her voice that she meant business. Ms. Gleason took the

note from Lucy. "Who wrote this?" she asked, looking around the room. "I'm waiting. Who wrote this?"

No one answered. Just nervous coughs and shuffling feet.

Ms. Gleason sat behind her desk. She ran her hand through her hair. "Well, I'm very upset. First, I'm going to see what I can do about this fish tank. I certainly hope that Bugs, Daffy, and Elmer are all right. As for the rest of you, take out your math booklets. I don't want to hear another sound for the rest of the day."

"But . . ." Helen started to say.

"Not a peep," said Ms. Gleason.

Chapter Eight
Dad's Amazing Raisins

We were pretty quiet on the bus ride home. Whenever Ms. Gleason was upset, we always felt worse.

"Oh, yeah, I almost forgot," I grumbled to Mila as we climbed off the bus. "My dad says he's taught the raisins a trick."

Mila snapped her head around. "What?! Is he serious?!"

I lifted my shoulders and let them droop. "You know my dad. He's never serious. It's probably some kind of magic trick. Come over after dinner," I told her. "We

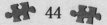

need to work on the case, anyway."

After dessert, my father cleared the table. We gathered around — Mom, Grams, Hillary, Daniel, Nick, Mila, and me. Even my dog, Rags, seemed interested. Though I think he was still hoping for scraps. Only my oldest brother, Billy, got up to leave.

"Don't you want to stay to see the swimming raisins?" my dad asked.

Billy waved his hand. "Thanks, but no thanks. But teach 'em how to fly on a tiny trapeze, and I'll pay money to see it."

"It's a deal," my dad answered, chuckling. He took out a bowl of raisins. Then he made a big show out of picking what he called "his five best swimmers."

He poured a large glass of seltzer. "And now, ladies and germs," he announced in a deep voice, "the amazing, terrific, fantabulous, swimming raisins!"

Hillary stifled a yawn.

My dad ignored her. He tossed the

raisins into the glass. "Come on, boys," he commanded. "Swim to Papa!"

Blub, blub, plop. Each raisin floated for a moment, then sank to the bottom.

"That's it?" Nick asked. "That's the trick? You taught them how to drown?"

My dad held up a hand. "Wait . . ."

One by one, the raisins stirred. Slowly, they rolled and jiggled and, finally, "swam"

back to the top of the glass. Then down again, then up, then down, and up again!

My dad stood and bowed. We all laughed and cheered.

"Those *are* amazing raisins," Mila said.

"It's the soda water," Daniel scoffed. "The bubbles make it work."

Mila didn't care. "I can't wait to try this at my house!" she exclaimed.

Chapter Nine

An Unexpected Twist

Mila and I went into my bedroom. I opened my detective journal. It read:

THE CRIMES
1. Green Jell-O in sneakers.
2. Rubber bologna in Joey's sandwich.
3. Tin of snakes for Mila.
4. Food coloring in fish tank.

I turned the page and showed Mila a picture I'd drawn. It was titled **"GOTCHA!"**

Mila frowned. "That doesn't look like me. It's more like the Bride of Frankenstein."

"You should have seen yourself when the snakes popped out," I said. "You *looked* like the Bride of Frankenstein!"

I walked around the room stiffly, with my arms outstretched, like Frankenstein's monster. We both cracked up. That's the thing about pranks. Sooner or later, they usually got a laugh.

"Do you still think it's Ralphie?" Mila asked.

I nodded. I ticked off the reasons on my fingers. "First, Ralphie is always joking. Second, you heard him on the bus. He's the

 49

one who's been laughing the loudest at all the pranks. Third, he had *opportunity*. He was on Cubby Patrol this week. I'm almost positive it's him."

"What do we do now?" Mila asked.

"We wait," I said.

"Wait?"

"Yeah," I said. "Ralphie should be over any minute."

"What?!" Mila screeched. "He's coming here? Now?"

I told Mila about my little plan. I gave her a piece of paper. We wrote our names in fat, round letters. Like this:

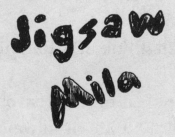

"We'll act like we're having a lot of fun," I told Mila. "Then we'll ask Ralphie to try it."

"Smart," Mila said, nodding. "We might get a match with the 'Gotcha' notes."

Rags barked at the front door. Then I heard my mother's voice. "You know the way, Ralphie. They're in the bedroom."

"Hey, guys," Ralphie greeted us. "What's going on?"

"We're writing our names in fat, round letters!" I announced. "It's so much fun! Try it!"

Mila eagerly shoved a paper and marker into Ralphie's hands.

Ralphie rolled his eyes. "Boring," he groaned. "Let's play Monopoly Junior instead."

Oh, well. It was time for Plan B. I took the direct approach. "I have to ask you a question, Ralphie. Are you the one playing all those pranks?"

Ralphie smiled nervously. A confused expression crossed his face. He looked at Mila, then back at me. "Are you *serious*?"

Our faces told him the answer.

"No way, Jigsaw! It's not me," he said.

"Do you promise?" I asked.

Ralphie promised.

"What about Cubby Patrol?" Mila wondered. "You were the only person who could have done some of those pranks."

Ralphie protested. "I wasn't on Cubby Patrol this week."

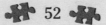

Mila raised an eyebrow. "You were listed on the board, Ralphie. I saw it."

Ralphie smiled. "Oh, that. I traded jobs with somebody. I got to clap the erasers instead."

"What?!" Mila and I said together.

"Yeah," Ralphie said, cracking a smile. "It was weird. Helen asked me if I'd switch jobs this week. I was, like, 'Sure!' Anybody would rather clap erasers than straighten up the cubbies."

"Helen Zuckerman," I murmured. "Go figure." I slid my eyes toward Mila. She looked so surprised, you could have knocked her down with a feather.

Ralphie explained, "Helen said she was allergic to chalk dust."

I stretched out my hand to Ralphie. "I want to apologize," I said. "I'm sorry I suspected you."

Ralphie waved the thought away. He couldn't care less. "Sorry? Are you kidding me? I *wish* I'd thought of that stuff. Pink food coloring in the fish tank — that's genius!"

I knew tomorrow would be a busy day. After Mila and Ralphie headed out, I got to bed nice and early. As usual, my dad read with me before tucking me in. We were in the middle of *Shiloh,* by Phyllis Reynolds Naylor. It was a really good story.

My dad closed the book and stood up to leave.

"Hey, Dad . . ."

"Yeah?"

"You were funny tonight, with the raisins."

He looked at me suspiciously. "Funny how?" he asked, rubbing his chin. "Funny strange? Or funny ha-ha?"

I smiled. "Just plain funny."

"Thanks, kiddo," he said, leaning down to kiss me. "I try."

Chapter Ten

In the Library

The next morning Mila and I talked it over at the bus stop. "Helen is the *last* person I would have suspected," Mila said.

"Tell me about it," I agreed. "I didn't think her skeleton *had* a funny bone. But we're a long way from catching her. We still need proof."

But getting proof wasn't going to be easy. All morning, I tried to find witnesses. I talked to so many kids my ears hurt.

No luck.

I even sneaked a peek at Helen's writing

folder. I was hoping to find a match with the "Gotcha" notes.

It was no luck all over again.

Poor Mila had it even worse. It was her job to hang around with Helen. Ask her tough questions. See if Mila could trick Helen into confessing. Instead, Helen just told Mila bad jokes all day.

By afternoon recess, we were pretty disappointed. Maybe it wasn't Helen after all.

Mila kicked a rock thoughtfully.

"Hey, wait a minute!" I exclaimed. "You know how Helen has been telling all those jokes lately?"

"Nonstop," Mila said, rolling her eyes. "Each one is worse than the next. She's been taking a lot of joke books out of the library."

"The library!" I exclaimed, "What if she read about *practical jokes,* too? I mean, let's face it. Helen's not funny. She has to get her ideas from somewhere."

"Yeah, so?" said Mila.

"So," I said, "follow me."

Ms. Gleason gave us permission to go to the library instead of taking recess.

The school librarian, Mrs. Kranepool, was a large, friendly lady. She wore her hair in a big lump at the top of her head. There were always a few pencils sticking out of it. "May I help you?" she asked kindly.

I told her we were working on a case.

Mrs. Kranepool slid her pointy glasses

down her nose. She peered over them. "A case? Is it very, very dangerous?"

"We just need information," I assured her.

"You've come to the right place," she answered. "Information is our specialty. Do you need help finding a book?"

"Um, not exactly." I pulled out my notebook. "Could you tell us what books Helen Zuckerman has taken out recently?"

Mrs. Kranepool's lips went tight. "Oh, dear," she said. "I'm afraid I can't do that."

"You mean, you don't know?" I was surprised. I thought librarians knew everything.

"It's not that," she replied. "But I'm afraid it's private information. That's Helen's business, not yours. I'm sure you understand."

I didn't. I told her that it was different for detectives. Other people's business *was* my business.

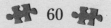 60

"I'm sorry, I can't help you," Mrs. Kranepool repeated. She began to type away at the computer.

Rats. We struck out.

Suddenly, Mila spoke up. "In that case, do you have any books on practical jokes?"

Mrs. Kranepool glanced at Mila. She pulled a pencil from her hair and tapped it against her open palm. "Practical jokes, hmmmm," she mused. "I seem to remember something. Try the humor section."

We tried. And we hit a grand slam. I pulled a book off the shelf: *Gross Gags and Practical Jokes,* by R. U. Nurvice.

In her excitement, Mila grabbed the book out of my hands, but it fell to the carpet. A paper slipped out of it. "Hey, somebody left a bookmark," Mila noticed. Then her eyes widened. "Look, Jigsaw."

She handed me the bookmark. There

were initials on it written in fat, balloonlike letters: **H.Z.**

"H.Z.!" I exclaimed. "Those are Helen's initials. She must have left this bookmark in here by accident."

"And check out the lettering," Mila observed. She pulled a piece of paper from her pocket. It read **GOTCHA!** in the same kind of lettering. The handwriting matched.

Mila flipped through the book. "Listen to this," she said, reading aloud.

There's nothing funnier than slime. Can't find any slime? Don't worry. Green Jell-O works just as well. When your friend isn't looking, place a hefty scoop of Jell-O in his or her shoe!

Mila turned a few more pages. She read again:

Food coloring is perfect for playing pranks. Take a wacky color and pour a few drops in your friend's milk. You can even put some in a fish tank! Don't worry, you won't hurt the fish. But you will get laughs from all your pals!

"These are the exact same pranks that happened in school," she said. "This means that . . ."

". . . we finally have our proof!" I said triumphantly.

Mila grinned. "I think it's time we gave Helen a taste of her own medicine."

Chapter Eleven

Gotcha!

Mila and I prepared a message in invisible ink. It was easy enough to do. We wrote the message by using a brush dipped in lemon juice. Then we told Athena what to do. The plan was set.

On Saturday afternoon, right on time, Helen Zuckerman came over to Athena's house. Athena led her into the playroom. Meanwhile, Mila, Joey, and I hid in a nearby closet. We left the door open a tiny crack and watched.

"So what's the big excitement?" Helen wondered.

Athena shoved a paper in front of Helen. "I found this secret message from Mila to Jigsaw," she said. "I bet it's about the case they're working on."

Helen looked sharply at Athena. "What case?"

"The practical joker," Athena said. "Jigsaw says they are hot on the trail."

Helen eyed the paper. "It's blank," she said. "There's nothing on it."

Athena shook her head. "That's because they used invisible ink. But I know how to read it."

Athena brought out a glass jar. She explained, "My mom helped me. It's just water mixed with a few drops of iodine." She handed Helen a small paintbrush. "You just brush it on, and the message magically appears."

Mila giggled quietly.

I poked her in the ribs. "Shhhh."

We could see that Helen was desperate to figure out what to do. Just as planned, Athena spoke up. "I've got to go to the bathroom," she said. "I'll be back in a few minutes."

Athena left Helen alone with the message.

We could see that Helen was worried. She didn't want to get caught. So of course she

couldn't read the message with Athena in the room. Quickly, Helen painted the iodine mixture on the page. The iodine turned the paper purple. The message written with lemon appeared in white. It read:

Gotcha Back!

Helen's face turned white.

She was caught, and she knew it.

This time, Mila couldn't help herself. She laughed out loud. A booming, rolling, rib-tickling laugh. The next minute, we all spilled into the room — laughing, pointing, and slapping one another on the back.

"Now *that's* funny!" I howled.

Helen frowned. Then slowly, as she watched our happy faces, she smiled, too. "I guess the joke's on me," she said.

There was one last detail. I put my hand

on Helen's shoulder. "I won't tell Ms. Gleason on you," I said. "Because I think it's something you should do yourself."

Helen nodded. "I already did," she confessed. "On Friday."

"Wow," Mila said. "That took guts. Was she mad?"

Helen tilted her head from side to side. "Not really. Ms. Gleason said she was glad that I was honest and told the truth. But she still gave me extra homework. I had to write out all the class rules — five times each!"

Helen glanced back at the paper. She looked at me. "I guess I deserved it," she admitted.

"Just one more thing," Mila said. "Why did you do it?"

Helen made a face. "I guess I wanted to be funny."

I didn't understand.

Helen continued, "Look at Ralphie. He's the most popular kid in class because he

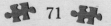

makes everyone laugh. I wanted to be popular, too."

"Helen, you don't have to be funny to make friends," Athena said. "You just have to be nice. And you're one of the nicest people I've ever met."

Helen's eyes beamed like two flashlights. Her smile filled the room. "Really?"

"Really," we all answered.

And that was that.

In a few minutes, Athena's mom came into the room. She was carrying a plate of brownies. Like magic, they vanished in a matter of minutes.

Me? I felt great, like I always did after solving a tough case. It took some work, and a lot of help from Mila. But I couldn't wait for the next case. After all, I loved mysteries.

And that's no joke.

Here's a sneak peek at the next

A JIGSAW JONES MYSTERY

The Case of the Detective in Disguise

by James Preller

Top Secret

The Detective Journal of Jigsaw Jones, Private Eye

Case: The Case of the Detective in Disguise

Client: Mike and Mary

Someone is stealing brownies from Mike and Mary's sandwich shop. Jigsaw is piecing together the clues—one crumb at a time. But no one is going to snatch a brownie with a detective watching. Time for Jigsaw to go undercover and catch this brownie bandit.